This book belongs to:

_____

To all the children in my life, may Santa always be magical for you, even when you are all grown up.

Books in the series...

Written by Katie Lorna McMillan
Illustrated by Graeme Andrew Clark
First printing 2018
ISBN 978-1-9997427-6-8
Published by Laughing Monkey Publishing

www.laughingmonkeypublishing.co.uk
email – info@laughingmonkeypublishing.co.uk

Find us on Facebook at
Haggis MacDougall – The mouse with a very long tail

For more illustrations by Graeme Andrew Clark,
visit - www.oldmangrey.com

Haggis MacDougall
saves Santa

Written by Katie Lorna McMillan
Illustrated by Graeme Andrew Clark

To Matthew
Enjoy the book!

My name is Haggis MacDougall. I have a very long tail for a mouse.

It helps me on my adventures, every time I leave the house.

My tail used to drive me mad, and left me feeling sad,

But now I think it is wonderful - it makes me really glad.

Well, here's my next adventure, are you listening girls and boys?

About the day I saved Christmas, helping Santa deliver the toys.

I can't wait to tell you my story,
you may find it hard to believe.

I'd just sat down with my cocoa,
on a snowy Christmas Eve.

The wind was howling loudly like the start of a snowstorm,

I was snuggled up in my jammies, and the fire was keeping me warm.

Suddenly, I heard a loud crash! I jumped up with such a fright.

I wanted to see what had happened, but it was dark at that time of night.

I picked up my flashlight, and shone it through my window.

All I saw was a pair of black boots, sticking out of the fresh fallen snow.

Now I really thought I was dreaming, as a man climbed out of the snow.

He had white hair, a beard, and dressed in red from head to toe.

His figure was plump, his cheeks were rosy, and his suit was trimmed in white.

I must admit, I'd never seen such a strange but magical sight.

Behind him there was a sleigh, filled high with colourful toys.

There were eight reindeer running around, making their reindeer noise.

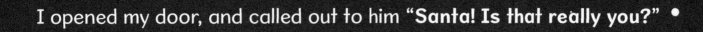

I opened my door, and called out to him "**Santa! Is that really you?**"

And a happy voice shouted back through the storm,
"**Haggis MacDougall, yes it's true!**"

Then Santa said...

"This snowstorm has ruined my sleigh full of toys.

I'm not sure what I'm going to do.

Do you think I could come into your little house,

While I think this problem through?"

"Of course Santa, please do come in!" I said, with a gleeful smile.

"I never dreamt I'd meet you, so please stay for a while.

Thank you for filling my stocking, every year on Christmas Eve.

You always enjoy the whisky and cookies that I leave."

"Ho, ho, ho!" said Santa happily, as he came into my house.

"This house is a little small for me, but perfect for a mouse.

"Oh my!" I said, "I'd love to help." I ran out to look at the sleigh.

The reins had snapped and broken off, the reindeer had run away.

"I can use my tail to act like the reins, so you can deliver these toys.

I want to help you save Christmas, for all the girls and boys."

"Wonderful Haggis, you are a star, your tail will save this night.

I'll put my reindeer back on this sleigh, we have a very long flight.

Dasher, Dancer, Prancer, Vixen, we have to leave right away!

Comet, Cupid, Donner, Blitzen, hurry we mustn't delay!"

I looped my tail through each reindeer hook, the sleigh looked as good as new.

Santa fed his reindeer magic oats, and up to the sky we flew.

I couldn't believe I was flying so high, with Santa by my side.

I was going to save Christmas, my heart was bursting with pride.

We stopped at every chimney, and Santa jumped off to deliver the toys.

I couldn't believe all the lovely presents, he'd made for the girls and boys.

At the end of the night, just as first light started to appear,

Santa delivered his last present, and whistled out to his reindeer.

'Whoo woo! Let's go with no time to spare, let's head to our North Pole home.

Haggis, my friend, since we need your tail, we hope you would like to come."

"Thank you Santa, I'd love to,
this journey has been the best.

I can't wait to meet Mrs Claus,
the elves and all the rest."

NORTH POLE

We arrived at his house, and Mrs Claus was waiting at the door.

She welcomed me in, and asked the elves to show me the toy store.

I saw how they made each little toy, and where the reindeer roam.

We fixed the reins of the sleigh, and then Santa flew me home.

So now this story has finished, I hope you enjoyed it all.

It's important to help out others, if their problem is big or small.

So, if someone needs your help, offer a helping hand (or tail).

It's always good to be kind in life, this is the moral of this tale.

 # The Haggis Quiz

1. What is Haggis doing in his house on Christmas Eve?

2. What noise does he hear outside?

3. Who was outside his house?

4. What had happened to Santa's sleigh?

5. Santa needs help from Haggis. What does he ask Haggis to do?

6. Does Haggis save santa?

7. Where does Santa live?

8. You can search for the robins throughout the book. Can you find them?

9. How many can you count?

For the answers to this quiz and more Haggis activities, please visit **www.laughingmonkeypublishing.co.uk**

Lightning Source UK Ltd.
Milton Keynes UK
UKHW05f0451150918
328912UK00006B/101/P